AF609441

MY GRANDPARENTS WERE DINOSAURS

MAGIC CAT PUBLISHING

First Published in 2025 by Magic Cat Publishing, an imprint of Lucky Cat Publishing Ltd,
Unit 2 Empress Works, 24 Grove Passage, London E2 9FQ, UK
EU Authorised Representative Magic Cat Publishing, an imprint of Lucky Cat Publishing Ltd,
PAKTA svetovanje d.o.o., Stegne 33, Ljubljana, Slovenia

A catalogue record for this book is available from the British Library.

ISBN 978-1-917044-15-8

The illustrations were created digitally
Set in Cafeteria

Published by Rachel Williams and Jenny Broom
Designed by Riko Sekiguchi
Edited by Jenny Broom

Manufactured in China

9 8 7 6 5 4 3 2 1

MY GRANDPARENTS WERE DINOSAURS

Anne and Steve Brusatte illustrated by Enrico Lorenzi

MAGIC CAT PUBLISHING

Hello! I don't think that I've met you before.
Now, you may not have heard,
I'm a REAL DINOSAUR.

So, before you start thinking I look like a meal...

Check my family tree –
and then see how you feel.

Our most famous relative you will all know...

My Uncle *T. REX* who lived long, long ago!
You think we look different?
Just check out our **feet**,

And our look-alike **feathers**...
Admit it, that's neat!

Old *Velociraptor* and *T. rex* and me
Belong to the same ***THEROPOD*** family.
Velociraptor
We strut on **two legs**,
we **swing** our arms free,
Spinosaurus

Ambopteryx
Some glide and some fly –
Caihong
like Caihong
... and ME!

The **first ever** feathers looked rather like hair.

For warming – *not flying* – is why they were there.

DEINONYCHUS used his rad wings for display,
He would show off to girls and **scare** rivals away.

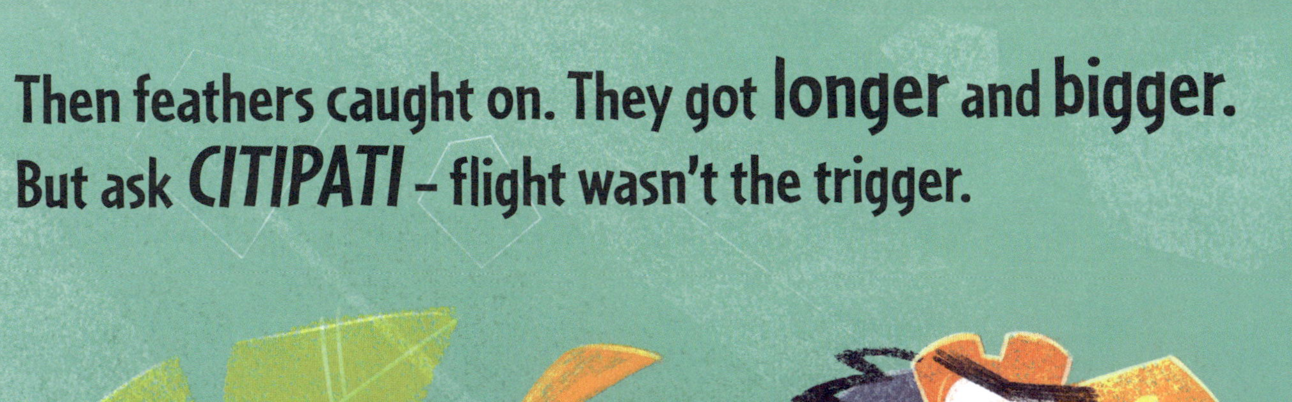

Then feathers caught on. They got **longer** and **bigger.**
But ask ***CITIPATI*** – flight wasn't the trigger.

My cousin used feathers to cover her **wings**
That **shielded** her eggs from dangerous things.

And speaking of wings, here's the lay of the land:
PTERODACTYLS? They're their very own band!
Sure, they had wings;
they could **fly**;
they could **soar**...

REALITY CHECK!
Not birds...
or dinosaurs.

You *still* don't believe me? **You really can't SEE?!**
How **chickens** fit into this family tree?
Then check this guy out. Don't rely on my word...
ARCHAEOPTERYX: the Original Bird.

My Jurassic Grandad had awesome curved claws,
A long, **feathery** tail and **sharp teeth** in his jaws.

Small wings...
Light bones... He flew just a bit,
Half-dino, half bird, this guy was a hit.

Meet Cousin *CAIHONG*,
she's from North-East China.

The fossil beds there... **Wow!**
There's just no place finer.

Lava helped Caihong stay super-preserved.
Her name, which means **'rainbow'**, you see is deserved!

Grandpa CONFUCIUSORNIS's tails
Were talk of the town with besotted females.

Chest muscles grew,
they got stronger and **stronger,**

And soon they could beat their
large wings for much longer.

Powerfully flapping them up and back down,
These dinosaur-birds started charting **new ground.**

Then, **sixty-six million years** before today
An asteroid hit. It was dino

Doooo

OMSDAY!

But some of our ancestors, clever and quick,
Who were not fussy eaters,
and had **tough little** chicks,

Crossed **deserts** and **mountains** – whatever was there –

Till they climbed and they perched
and they **swam** everywhere!

Giant-sized penguins grew more than **two metres**,
these bullet-shaped swimmers were deadly fish eaters.

Falcon's ancestors shrieked terrible shrieks,
While hummingbird's grandparents grew narrow beaks.

Now, there are
TEN THOUSAND SPECIES,
I've heard,

From big Cousin Ostrich,
to wee Hummingbird.

So, when someone tells
you the dinos are gone,
You can inform them they're
totally wrong.

And as for your plan
to make short work of me...

You'd better check first with my BIRD FAMILY!

TRUE STORY!

The first dinosaurs lived about 230 million years ago, in the Triassic Period, when all land was joined together into a single 'supercontinent' called Pangea. These first dinosaurs were only the size of cats and dogs. They stood on all fours, ran quickly and ate both meat and plants. Dinosaurs can be divided into three major groups:

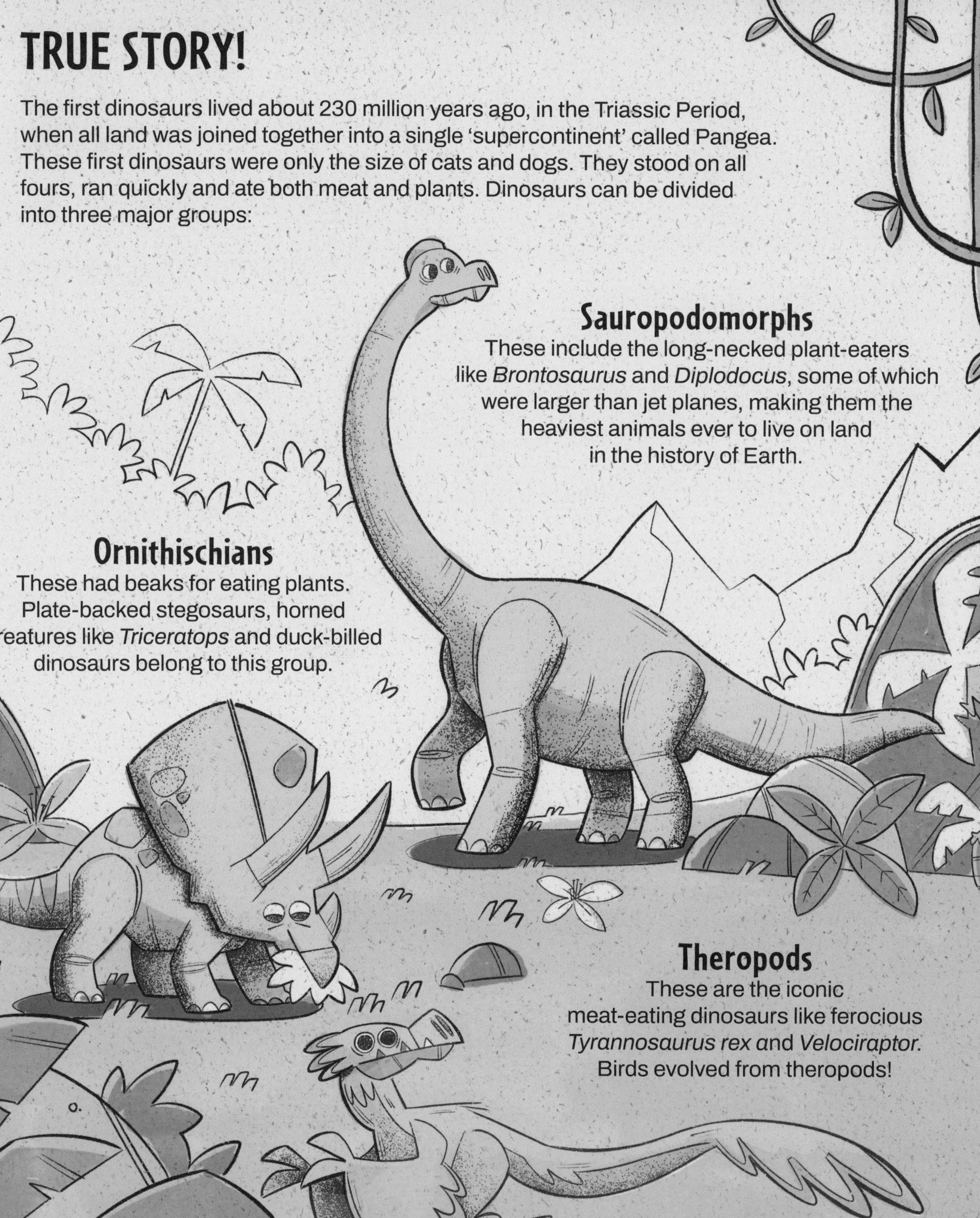

Sauropodomorphs

These include the long-necked plant-eaters like *Brontosaurus* and *Diplodocus*, some of which were larger than jet planes, making them the heaviest animals ever to live on land in the history of Earth.

Ornithischians

These had beaks for eating plants. Plate-backed stegosaurs, horned creatures like *Triceratops* and duck-billed dinosaurs belong to this group.

Theropods

These are the iconic meat-eating dinosaurs like ferocious *Tyrannosaurus rex* and *Velociraptor*. Birds evolved from theropods!

13 metres (roughly 43 feet)

Tyrannosaurus rex is probably the most famous dinosaur of all. *T. rex* lived about 66 million years ago in western North America. *T. rex* was one of the largest pure meat-eaters ever. It was about 13 metres (43 feet) long, weighed seven tons and had a head the size of a bathtub. It used its 50 banana-sized teeth to bite through the bones of its prey. As strange as it seems, *T. rex* is a close cousin of birds, although birds evolved from smaller theropods like the turkey sized *Velociraptor* – not giants like *T. rex*.

Scientists in the 1860s first proposed that birds evolved from dinosaurs. Why did they think this?

It was because the skeletons of small, meat-eating theropod dinosaurs like *Compsognathus* look very similar to the skeletons of birds. For example, today's birds and the extinct theropods walk only on their hindlegs, have extra backbones linking their hips to their bodies, and have feet with three big toes. No other animals, living or dead, share all of these features.

For many decades, scientists debated whether birds really did evolve from dinosaurs. Some scientists did not believe it. But then, in the 1990s, remarkable new fossils were found in China: dozens of dinosaurs covered in feathers. Only birds today have feathers. This proved once and for all that today's birds are part of the dinosaur family.

Why did it take so long for palaeontologists to find feather-covered dinosaur fossils?

It's because feathers are soft things that grow out of the skin. Usually feathers break down quickly once a bird (or dinosaur) dies. But around 125 million years ago in China, many dinosaurs were rapidly buried by volcanic eruptions, which turned the feathers to fossils. Since the first feathered dinosaur fossil was found in 1996, thousands more have been discovered!

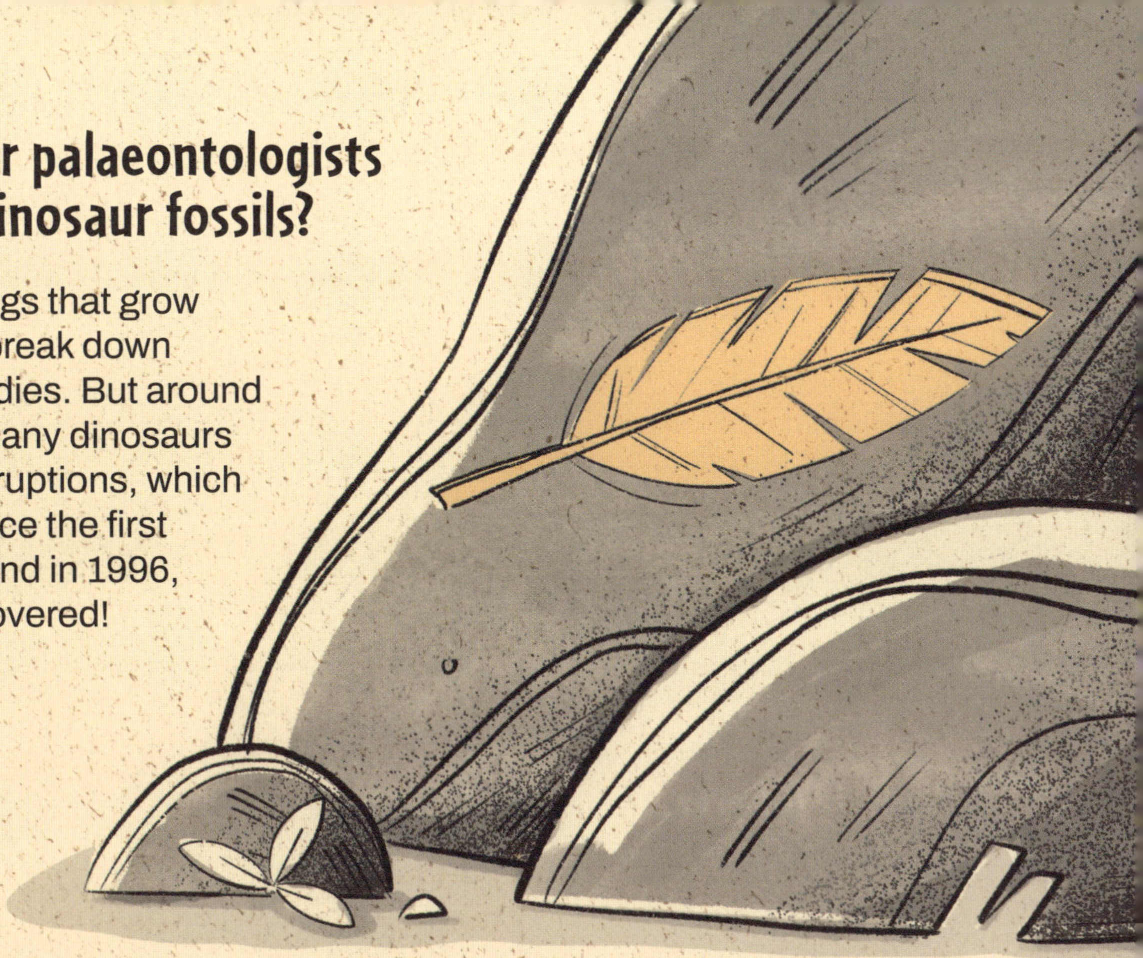

Evolution of feathers

Many dinosaurs had feathers sticking out of their skin. But most of the time, these feathers were simple little ribbons that looked like hair. There is no way that these small feathers could have been used for flying. Instead, palaeontologists think that feathers first evolved for the same reason hair developed in mammals: to keep these dinosaurs warm.

In some meat-eating dinosaurs, like *Velociraptor*, their simple hair-like feathers evolved into more complicated structures. The feathers got longer and bushier, and lined up on the arms to form wings. But, the first wings were too small to be used for flying. Instead, they were probably used for display. You can think of them as billboards, for attracting mates or scaring away rivals!

In the Jurassic period, about 150 million years ago, some of these feathery dinosaurs like *Archaeopteryx* began flapping their wings. Their wings became big enough to generate two powerful forces. First is lift, which moves an animal upwards. And second is thrust, which moves an animal forward. Now these dinosaurs could fly! True birds had evolved from dinosaurs.

The first birds were probably not very good at flying. They could only stay in the air for a short amount of time and not travel very far. But then some birds, like *Confuciusornis*, developed huge muscles on their chests, which they used to beat their wings faster.

There were many species of birds flying over the heads of *T. rex*, *Triceratops* and other dinosaurs in the Cretaceous period. Then, 66 million years ago, there was a terrible catastrophe. A huge asteroid from outer space slammed into the Earth, causing fires, earthquakes and floods. Most animals died, including all of the big dinosaurs. But some of the birds survived, probably because they could fly away from the danger.